ROPED

PURGATORY CLUB

E.M. GAYLE

GYPSY INK BOOKS

eliza@emgayle.com
http://EMGayle.com
Eliza on Twitter
Eliza on Facebook
Eliza on Goodreads
Eliza on Instagram
Sign up for Eliza's Newsletter

* * *

Welcome to Purgatory! A club for every desire...

Katie has a thing for rope and she's had her eye on riggers Leo and Quinn for quite some time. Week after week she goes to the club and watches them tie up women from afar, while she imagines their rough rope against her own skin.

Now the two hunky men have decided to make their move. But is plus-sized Katie ready to turn her fantasies into reality?

CHAPTER 1

Katie watched Leo's hands stroke the woman's inner thigh with the rope as he tied it around her leg. She imagined the course texture scraping against her own sensitive skin, sending a shiver snaking along her spine. She continued to observe the twists and turns of the rope as they wrapped it around both her legs and waist. The girl giggled through the process but the lines etched in Leo's face showed just how serious he took his job. The loud beat of industrial music playing in the club pounded with her own heartbeat, pulsating through her body. Bodies crushed around her as the night's play got into full swing, but her attention remained solely on the rope.

She tuned it all out to focus on the station below. Soon both Leo and Quinn would hook the woman up to the swing and fling her across the club, but first he tied her. Wetness pooled between her thighs with the familiar longing to be the girl in Leo's hands, slowly tied from limb to limb until her freedom was stripped and her trust tested.

"Isn't it about time you quit watching and started feeling, Katie?" The familiar timber of Quinn's voice whispered in her ear as his arms grabbed the railing on either side of her, trapping her in his embrace. Her pulse skipped as she sucked in a shallow breath of surprise. "That could be you down there, feeling the rope across your belly, wrapped around your wrists and totally at his mercy."

Her nipples peaked against her shirt at the mere image his words brought to mind. She screwed her eyes closed tight, as she tried to stop the effect he was having on her.

"Shouldn't you be down there helping out your partner?" She tried to concentrate on her breathing but the man pressed against her back made her heart race and her body burn with renewed need. The heat alone was enough to make her weak in the knees.

"Come with me, Katie. Let me tie you."

She shook her head as fear gripped her body. She wasn't ready. She wasn't sure she could recover from either Leo or Quinn teasing her body like that.

Quinn grasped her wrist and flipped her around to face him. His amber eyes pierced through her with a heated intensity as he watched her reactions. "You come here week after week and stand here looking down at us as we work. Do you think we don't notice the longing on your face? The way your body squirms as we wrap more and more rope around the girls who ask us to? Why are you torturing yourself? Or should I say...what are you waiting for?"

She closed her eyes to his questions, searching for an adequate answer when she knew there was none. How could she deny the truth? "I admire your work. What's wrong with that?"

His fingers gently grasped her chin and tilted her head back, forcing her to look at him. "We see you,

Katie, we know what you need. Why do you hide here?"

She bristled against his words, shame heating her face. "I'm not hiding, Quinn, I'm just observing. I'm here and I'm alone, yet no one ever approaches or speaks to me. Which is fine, but don't tell me that I'm hiding. What am I supposed to do? Throw myself at someone?"

A grin split Quinn's handsome face, revealing the beautiful smile she loved so much. She always noticed how happy his job made him and she envied him that feeling. Some ties were more intense than others as evidenced by the hard lines of his face when he concentrated or the occasional bulge in his pants when a willing female turned him on. It was those moments when she had fleeting thoughts of both him and Leo taking her for their own. The popular riggers were frequently gossiped about around Purgatory, and word was they had a great time playing the scene together but hadn't taken a submissive of their own for a very long time.

"You don't have to get defensive with me, babe. I'm not sure what's wrong with the men in this club, letting you spend all your time alone. Their loss is my gain, though." He leaned closer, his lips a breath away from her own. The sharp tang of citrus filled her nostrils and she imagined he'd just come from a break where he would have eaten an orange. Did he realize even the way his hands peeled the skin from an orange could turn a woman inside out?

Katie sucked in a slow breath, afraid to move. She worried he would kiss her as much as she worried that he wouldn't. She was in a mood tonight, and watching the play stations hadn't helped but instead stoked the flames inside her until, now pressed against one of the men of her nightly dreams, she wanted nothing more than to submit to his every whim. She ached with the desire to be touched, to be tied, and to be fucked by Quinn and Leo.

He edged a little closer, but instead of kissing her like she expected, he stroked her lips with his tongue. A gentle touch that was more like a taste than a kiss. He leaned into her until they were pressed together from hips to breast, and his erection was unmistakable pushed against her belly and pelvis. His hot tongue licked at the corner of her mouth and along the seam of her lips. She opened farther on a soft sigh but he only continued his exploration.

Her own arousal went off the charts as she rolled her hips against his. A low growl sounded in his throat and he pulled his head back from hers. "Careful, Katie. For a girl who professes to being happy alone, your body is quickly making a liar out of you."

She clamped her mouth shut and tried to pull back, but there was nowhere to go. He had her against the railing and his arms still held her in place. "I think we should stop this, people are starting to stare."

Quinn glanced to the side, looking at the crowd surrounding them. "Since when do crowds bother either of us? That's common around here and no one really cares what we do. In fact, they probably wish we would do more. I think inside everyone here lies the heart of a voyeur."

She couldn't argue with that. Even she got excited watching some of the activities going on in the private play area. Especially the flogging. It had been so long since a flogger kissed her skin she might not remember the sensation, but every time she came to the club and watched, she got turned on as hell seeing the red streaks on bare flesh after a session in a booth. She enjoyed every flinch and emotion that crossed the faces of the submissives.

She loved the crackling sound of leather slapping a bare back or bottom. Oh yeah, she had it bad tonight, and there was never a shortage of people willing to put on a show.

"I can admit I enjoy watching, but I'm not sure I want to be the one on display."

The corner of his mouth turned up in a wry smile at her words. "We'll see about that." He pushed away from her and grasped her hand. "Come with me."

She looked down at his hand covering hers. The heat and desire enveloped her further from the simple movement. His rope roughened hands scraped against her wrist, igniting a flame deep inside her belly, the kind of thing that she hadn't felt in a very long time.

"Where are we going?"

"I have to get back to work and I don't want you far. I wasn't kidding when I said it was time."

Not giving her a chance to answer, he turned and pulled her into the crowd. Warm and pulsing bodies rubbed against her as they made their way through the throng of people clustered around the play stations. When they passed by the last St. Andrew's cross, a glance to the left showed her a new girl getting flogged by Dan, a Dominant who more than knew what he was doing. She was bare from the waist up and there were a variety of red, criss-crossing welts on her naked back. Despite Quinn leading her, she slowed her pace enough to take a look at the girl's face. Her black hair partially covered her features, but Katie managed to catch a glimpse of cobalt blue eyes glittering with tears. Despite the tears, or because of them, the naked emotion glowed from her face.

Katie's breath hitched in her throat when their gazes locked, and she understood exactly the ecstasy the woman experienced. With the dazed look in her eyes and the relaxed state of her body as she hung cuffed to the cross, it became obvious she was far beyond the simple pleasure of the leather striking her skin. She'd made it to the happy place affectionately called sub space.

A surge of envy rushed through her as she tore her gaze from the girl and refocused on Quinn in front of her. His sandy brown hair just brushed his shoulders and curled at the ends, and she imagined it to have a silky texture that would glide through her fingers like water. The snug black t-shirt that he wore hugged his broad shoulders and back before tapering down to disappear into the dark jeans wrapped around a tight ass and legs. That picture alone was enough to make any girl drool. She'd had her eye on Quinn for a very long time.

As they approached the stairs that would take them down to Leo and the ropes, her belly fluttered with nerves and an obvious case of fear. She really wasn't sure if she could do this, especially here in front of so many people who knew her as a regular.

When she first came to the club, she had wanted to learn more about the lifestyle and even dared to hope that she would find someone who might want to teach her. And learned she had, by watching and even sometimes suffering through her own arousal to all the stimuli in the room. But other than the staff, who had been warm and friendly to her, not a single man had approached her.

Looking at many of the beautiful, rail thin women of the club, she'd been forced to admit that her plus-size figure might not measure up for most of the men here. But she had no intention of letting that deter her from enjoying the atmosphere of the club and spending a few hours a week with like-minded people who at least wouldn't consider her thoughts and desires perverse or disgusting like her ex did.

"Katie, are you okay?"

She jerked her head up, surprised to find herself standing next to Quinn and Leo's private table and Quinn's gaze boring into hers with concern.

"Yeah—uhm—I'm fine." She tamped down her nervousness as best she could and gave him a small smile.

"Good, then you can sit here and watch while you wait, if you would like."

She looked at the table of women all waiting for their turn at the ropes and her stomach fluttered all over again. She didn't want to be one of their groupies, she just wanted to watch. This up close and personal, she didn't think she could hide just how turned on she would get. Nor did she want to be compared to the bevy of women who hovered here, hoping they would get picked next.

"Quinn—I'm not so sure—"

He pressed his fingers to her lips to quiet her words. "I am sure and Leo is sure. You have to start trusting sometime, Katie." With that he turned and walked over to the platform to join Leo in tying up their latest volunteer for the swing. Leo glanced over to her and smiled at Quinn with the wickedest looking grin she had ever seen. The kind of *oh, shit* look that made her realize how serious they were about this.

Two hours later, Katie still waited at the table but had begun fidgeting in the chair. Her fingers tapped out the rhythm of the song playing through the club against the edge of the table, and her gaze darted everywhere in an attempt to not look at the ropes. Quinn and Leo had tied girl after girl without another word to her and her patience had run out. She wanted to either scream in frustration about being left waiting so long or stomp from the club like a child. She'd told Quinn that she wasn't ready for this yet, but he and Leo had apparently been discussing her at length. She'd watched and waited for weeks and couldn't be more surprised that they'd done the same. But this waiting was killing her.

She wanted to let her guard down and give them a chance, but the longer she sat there thinking about it the more she wanted to bolt. Doubts continued to plague her as she watched each new girl approach them. Why would they want to be the ones to teach her? It had been far easier to stay on the sidelines at a good distance and just observe. She glanced down at her cell phone for the umpteenth time to check the clock. Things would be winding down before long, so maybe they wouldn't put her on display. She could hope.

Earlier in the evening when she walked through the VIP doors, the first person she'd noticed was Leo leaning against a barstool dressed in a navy blue tee and looking through the crowd with a watchful eye. She couldn't resist staring at him. She'd heard many women in the club say that his bald head and tribal tattoo around his neck made him look scary. She couldn't disagree more. The man was sexy as sin from top to bottom. Given half the chance, she'd rub all over him like a cat in heat.

When he caught her watching him she had immediately become self-conscious. Maybe wearing her new slim skirt and a simple black corset hadn't been such a great idea. She had decided to leave her hair down tonight, thinking the red of it against the pale color of her skin and the dark as night corset would look good. She brushed her hands down the fabric covering her torso—she loved the new corset she'd bought. It made her feel feminine, not to mention it took several inches off her waist. If she hadn't known better she could have sworn the look in Leo's eyes said she looked good enough to eat.

"You look really nervous sitting there. Have you never done this before?"

Katie looked at the woman sitting across the table. "No, this is my first time."

"You don't have anything to worry about. Quinn and Leo there know just how to handle a woman."

The way the words rolled from the woman's mouth sounded like experience, and sexy as hell. The dreamy look in her eyes as she watched the two men grated on Katie's nerves. She so didn't belong here.

She glanced again at the time, then at the tiny blonde woman with enormous silicone tits that were completely bare except for two X's of black tape covering her generous nipples. The club would be closing soon, making the blonde the last customer of the night.

So much for it being her time.

She shook her head and turned back to the woman at the table. "Yes, I just bet they do."

The woman must have caught the sarcasm in her response because she swung her head to look at Katie with a sharp, laughing look in her eyes.

"They have been eyeing you for a long time, sweetie, just waiting for you to be ready."

"Uh huh."

She flashed a quick smile. "You have no idea what you're in for, do you? Well, I guess it doesn't really matter. They'll be sure to let you know when they are good and ready. The question you have to ask yourself is, are you ready?" She stood and walked away from the table and up to Leo and Quinn. She kissed them both soundly on the mouth and told them good luck. She stopped again at the table on her way to the door. "Tonight you are the envy of every woman in the club."

She walked through the exit, leaving Katie in a state of shock.

Leo leaned over the girl attached to the rope swing between them and spoke to Quinn. Whatever he said made him look over at her, and she fought not to squirm under his gaze. Quinn laughed and left the platform and headed directly for her.

Uh oh.

He dismissed the other women at the table and seated himself next to Katie.

"Having fun?" He took a swig of water from the bottle he'd left on the table earlier.

"Not really. Your groupies are the most boring women I have ever met. Although just calling them women is a stretch."

He couldn't hold back a smile on that one. She'd hit the nail on the head and not even he could deny it. Not many women who came to Purgatory and lined up for the rope swing were really all that affected by the touch of the rope, at least not that she could see. Instead they were just looking for a cheap thrill.

"Leo and I have learned to tune them out. You do get used to it after a while." He leaned in closer, enough to whisper in her ear. "You're fidgeting, Katie. Why?"

"I thought you brought me down here to be tied into the swing."

"You thought we were going to do that here?" Leo's voice sounded from over Quinn's shoulder.

"Well—uhm—yeah, I guess so." Feeling embarrassed, she hoped her face wasn't as red as she thought.

"I might not have been completely clear as to when..."

"What do you mean?" She whispered the question, anger filling her as she spoke. She uncrossed her legs and moved to stand—it was time to go. She'd thought to offer them her submission, but for some reason they simply wanted to humiliate her.

Leo placed his hands on her shoulder and took the seat behind her. "Your first time shouldn't be in public, but it should be now and with us. Do you really want to deny it? You should probably think about that before answering me. I expect you to be honest with yourself as well as with us. Anything else will be met with punishment."

Katie's cheeks flushed hot at Leo's words as she stumbled with a response. "I—I—would never be dishonest."

"That's not what I meant and you know it, sweetheart. You have a good heart, but you hide behind your wall. You want to submit but you won't open yourself up to it." Leo's fingers tapped along her shoulders, rubbing the bare flesh. "But that's what we're here for. We are both going to ask a lot of you tonight, are you prepared for that? Do you want it?"

Her gaze lifted and met Quinn's directly as she struggled with the irritation and fear. His laughter had been replaced with an intensity that took her breath away and made it difficult to look at him.

Katie glanced again at Quinn but focused on Leo touching her. She'd waited so long to hear the words, she wasn't sure she could believe them. Yes, she wanted them, but would she ever be the same again afterwards?

Leo was right, though, her own issues prevented her from giving in and really she just needed to relax and live a little.

"I'm scared."

"If you weren't I don't think either of us would be talking to you. We both take your submission very seriously." Leo continued to massage and stroke her shoulders and she damn near melted into his skillful hands, it felt so good. They'd kept her on edge for hours and she'd soaked her panties in anticipation of their touch. Now here they were, and they were giving her one last chance to back out. She wasn't going to take it.

"I'm sure." Her quiet, simple statement brought out a wicked grin on Quinn's face, and Leo pressed his lips to the back of her neck while his hands continued to roam her arms and torso.

"I can't wait to get you out of this corset and tie you up for myself." Leo's words sent a quick pulse straight to her already tight nipples and renewed heat pooled between her thighs.

When Quinn leaned forward and placed his hands on her knees, she nearly shot out of the chair. His touch electrified her.

"Spread your legs for me, Katie," he demanded.

Surprised by the sudden changes of the two men, she hesitated before letting her legs fall slightly apart, giving Quinn the access he sought. Grateful she'd taken the time to pamper her body before she came to the club, she held her breath as his fingers slid up her thighs and underneath the hem of her skirt.

"Are you wet, sweetheart?" She shivered at the kiss of Leo's warm breath on her skin as he spoke to her again, trying to distract her from the fact that Quinn was scant inches away from her pussy.

"Yes." Her husky answer gave away just how aroused she was, but did little to relieve the tension building or the wanting for them to hurry up and get on with it. In fact, she was beginning to care less and less about being in public, which gave her a better understanding as to why so many submissives in the club went so far in their play with others watching. At some point during the play there comes a time, she knew, when you don't care about anything but feeling. Something that no amount of research or observation could make someone understand.

She closed her eyes and held her breath when Quinn grazed the soft fabric between her legs. She bucked her hips toward his hand and a small groan escaped her lips.

"Oh yeah, Leo, she's ready. So fucking wet and hot." His fingers pushed aside her panties and slid through her slick folds, glancing across her swollen clit. She whimpered in pleasure as Leo grabbed her chin and twisted her head to the side so he could capture her lips in a hungry and demanding kiss. Pleasure arrowed through her as one man teased her clit and the other kissed her senseless. Losing focus, her instincts took over and her body began to build toward an orgasm. When she didn't think she could hold it back, she tore her mouth from Leo and pleaded for more.

"No, baby, not yet." With that statement Quinn gave her clit a hard little pinch that took not only her breath but also quelled her impending orgasm. Moments later she panted for air and her eyes watered with threatening tears. "Just breathe, Katie, in through your nose and out of your mouth. Open your eyes and look at me."

She did open her eyes and looked around to see several people watching her display before settling her gaze on Quinn. Her body flushed hotly with embarrassment as he withdrew his hand and resettled her skirt back in place.

"I think we're done here and it's time to go home." For a minute she thought Leo meant they were done with her and wanted her to go on her way, but then he stood and grabbed her hand to pull her along with him. "Give your keys to Quinn so he can follow us with your car, you're going home with us."

She didn't argue, she couldn't. Her body raged with need and a desire for these two men like never before. She figured even one night of pleasure with the elusive men would last her a very long time, and she wasn't about to turn it down.

CHAPTER 3

Surprised by how quickly they arrived at their place, she became fascinated with the one-room loft in the industrial area of downtown. The large space was essentially split in half with a small open-air kitchen and large living area filled with leather couches and chairs and enough electronics to make any Best Buy geek jealous. At each end of the room were large, king-sized beds covered with black suede comforters and a couple of chest of drawers. The walls were covered with framed black and white prints of women in various states of undress and tied in every possible position an imagination could think of.

But it was the idea that the two of them lived together with no privacy from the other that intrigued her the most. She'd often wondered if they were lovers as they seemed so in sync with each other, not to mention all the stories she'd heard about them sharing women when they played. Did they share each other when there weren't any women around? An image of their naked bodies writhing on one of those beds together flashed through her mind and she let out a low moan.

"Are you okay, Katie?"

She jerked her head to meet Quinn's gaze as her heart beat faster at being caught in a dark fantasy she wasn't about to share with anyone.

"Hmm. Wouldn't I like to know what you were just thinking of? "

"I'm—uhm—no." She pushed those crazy thoughts from her brain and concentrated on her surroundings once again. "Nice place you have here. Suits you both."

"Thanks, we like it." Quinn led her further into the loft, next to the seating area. Leo took a seat on one of the couches directly in front of her and Quinn walked around behind her, leaving her to face Leo with him at her back. His fingers went to the laces of her corset and slowly began to loosen them. Her body heaved a sigh of relief as she inhaled a deep, relaxing breath.

"That's it, Katie, relax and let Quinn work his magic."

She loved the rough, dark timbre of Leo's voice—its inherent power soothed her rough edges. She smiled and continued her deep breaths.

"Yes, Sir."

"Now that's more like it." His hands rubbed against his jeans-covered thighs slowly, up and down their length. Her gaze immediately went to the growing bulge in his lap, which she tried to avert her eyes away from but couldn't. Instead she thought only of kneeling there on the floor before him and freeing his erection so she could suck him. Her mouth watered with desire to know his taste. To feel his hand on her head as he fucked her mouth.

Oh, dear God, she was so horny.

"We know you've heard of safe, sane, and consensual. Do you have a safe word?"

She shook her head.

"Okay then for tonight you will use the word 'red.' If you use it, all play will stop. Understood?"

"Yes, Sir." Although stopping was the furthest thing from her mind.

Quinn drew out her laces one by one before he finally finished releasing her from the corset and whisked it off her body and tossed it into an empty chair. Cool air rushed across her skin and her nipples pebbled instantly. Strong, masculine fingers traced the indented curve of her waist before sliding up her rounded stomach to cup a plump breast in each hand. She sighed in pure ecstasy at his touch.

"Have you ever had your breasts bound?"

"No." Her answer came out barely a whisper. She found it hard to talk when she couldn't even think. Her body felt like it was on fire and her pussy creamed harder in response. The scent of her heat filled the air around them and she was certain they could both smell it.

"There are so many ways I can work the rope around you, it's hard to pick just one." Leo's fingers pulled and strummed her aching nipples as he spoke. A sigh escaped her lips as she arched into his hands, praying he wouldn't stop.

"Take off your skirt." With shaky fingers she fumbled with the button and the zipper before shimmying the skirt down her hips and thighs. Leo scooped her skirt from the floor and tossed it out of the way.

"Do you have a favorite design?" She suspected that some of the Shibari patterns would be, and she could imagine how sensual he would make her look and feel tied up in one.

His hands dropped to her side and he took a step away from her. She looked at Leo in alarm, who with a simple look reassured her everything was fine.

Quinn walked over to a tall cabinet in the corner and opened the front panel to reveal row after row of coiled rope in every color imaginable.

"This is our private rope collection, Katie. Each one has been hand colored with a specific person or design in mind. He reached in to the top shelf and removed an exquisite magenta colored strand and moved back toward her. "This is the one we designed specifically for you, babe. We've been saving it."

"You were that sure of me?" Quinn merely smiled. "You planned tonight?"

"We've been planning tonight for a long time, sweetheart. We just had to wait until we thought you were ready."

She shivered a little from the cold and from the confidence that these two men had in her. Could she possibly live up to it? "And you think I'm ready now?"

"Yes." They replied in unison.

Quinn unfurled the rope and draped it over her shoulders. The dark burgundy color against her fair skin stood out stark and beautiful. They were right about it being a good color for her.

Her favorite dress was in that exact shade. In fact, last month she'd worn that sexy outfit to the club and Leo had complimented her on it.

Leo stood from the couch and paced toward her, stopping mere inches from her nude body. His fingers grabbed the edges of the rope and pulled her forward against him as he slanted his mouth across hers. His tongue plunged through her lips, taking her with an unexpected hunger. Her own body responded as she rubbed against him, spreading her legs just enough for the rough fabric of his pants to scrape against her clit. She moaned into his mouth as he pulled the rope tighter, forcing it to dig into the skin on the back of her neck.

Hands grasped at the globes of her ass, spreading them, and a finger ran along the crack. She'd never had two men touching her at the same time, and their attention was a heady sensation as they pinched, pulled, and prodded her sensitive spots. Every movement came with a spark of both pain and pleasure as they experimented with her body.

When Leo pulled from her lips she wanted to beg and plead for more, but she instinctively knew better. Two experienced Dominants working her body were only going to give her what they wanted and nothing more. She had to be patient. He tied a knot into the rope at her throat, which rested in the hollow like a necklace. Leo continued to make a series of knots at short intervals all the way to the apex between her thighs.

Quinn's hands moved across her back and under her arms to her front. When he wrapped a separate section of rope between the knots that Leo had tied and pulled them tight around her back, it created a diamond pattern on her chest. He tied off the rope and repeated the process with each new section until she had a series of diamonds trailing down her torso straight to her pussy. Occasionally the last knot rubbed against her clit, causing her to lose her breath and focus every damn time.

With a wicked smile Leo bent down to pull the rope between her legs. She'd seen this pattern before and she knew they would attach the rope work in the front to what Quinn had done in the back and, oh dear God, that rope would nestle between her folds and run up her ass to her back.

Already her body flamed hot. The scrapes and tugs of the ropes against her skin drove her mad, and she just knew that if that knot rubbed her just a little bit more she would explode.

On the verge of begging to come, Katie cried out when Leo buried his face between her legs. His tongue speared the slick, heated folds, licking at her juice but not touching her swollen clit. Instead he slid downward and plunged his tongue inside her as deep as he could get it. Her head lolled backwards against Quinn's chest as he braced her arms with his hands to keep her from falling.

"Whatever you do, Katie, don't come without permission."

CHAPTER 4

*W*as he kidding? She wanted to scream in frustration as she tried to wriggle away from Leo's tempting tongue. Her attempts to stop him were futile. He simply grabbed her ass and held her tight against his face, while he continued to work her pussy with his hot tongue. She wanted to cry. Their demand for her to not come under these conditions was unreasonable. She wouldn't—couldn't hold back.

"I—I can't stop it. Please, please, it's..."

Her words died as Quinn pinched her nipples so hard it took her breath away. The demanding need to come died with the onset of such sharp, unexpected pain. Tears sprang to her eyes.

"Don't worry, babe, if you can't control it, I will." His firm words settled around her like a blanket. He and Leo had every intention of taking their pleasure as needed but, just as important, they would take care of her. In that moment they were everything to her and that warm feeling not only eased her pain but left her with the desire to please them like never before.

With a few last frenzied licks to her over sensitized tissues, Leo not only brought her right back to the brink of orgasm but he pulled away from her then, denying her a release.

Her gaze latched onto his at the sight of him licking his lips. "Such a good girl. Tastes good too," Leo spoke as he threaded the rope between her soaked flesh, turning it over to Quinn, who pulled it tight enough so that the texture of the rope touched every sensitive spot she could think of. Quinn settled the last knot snugly against her hard little clit.

If she moved even a tiny fraction, teasing pleasure fractured through her, which was designed precisely to drive her crazy. When the rope was secure, Quinn delivered a sharp little blow to her ass. "Now the real fun can begin. But first, don't you want to see how gorgeous you look now? Tied just for us?"

"Yes." It was all she could manage. Even deep breathing moved the rope enough to excite her.

He grabbed her hand and pulled her behind him. A gasp of pleasure forced its way from her mouth with each step. The simple movement of one step in front of another moved the tight rope along her pussy and ass, a constant press and release of pure bliss that made it difficult to think.

"Feels so good, doesn't it?" She nodded. "You're not going to come until I tell you to, right?"

"Yes, Sir."

He stopped her in front of a full-length mirror that gave her a first glimpse of her rope-clad body. Normally a little self conscious about her nudity, what they'd done to her, the beautiful rope work, made her proud of the way she looked.

"Oh my God, it's stunning!" She tried to fight back the tears that welled in her eyes, but a few leaked out anyway. "You've made me so beautiful."

Both men stepped closer and embraced her between them.

"No, Katie, you were already beautiful beyond measure, we just showed you how much."

"I don't know what to say," she whispered. "Thank you."

"Don't thank us yet, let's see how you feel when we are done playing with you."

A healthy dose of fear shot through her, but not enough to bring her back from the euphoria they had created. She felt so good right now, she almost didn't care what they did as long as she got to come soon.

"Do you still remember your safe word?" She nodded. "What is it? I need you to say it."

"Red."

"Okay then, go get up on that bench then and get down on all fours for us, baby."

She looked over to where Leo pointed and saw a black leather padded bench only a few feet away. She took a deep breath to steady herself because she knew even a few feet of movement could be enough to make her come, and she couldn't do that until they said.

She moaned with agonizing pleasure when she moved toward the bench, the continued rubbing against her sensitive flesh almost more than she could bear.

Her steps faltered. "Please."

"Almost, baby. Just do as you're told and we'll take care of you. Trust in that." She heard the rustling of clothes being removed behind her as she took the last few steps and got into position as requested. With her ample ass high in the air and nothing to cover herself, feelings of vulnerability mixed with pure decadence washed through her. She watched both men approach her, Leo carrying a crop and Quinn a wicked grin.

She stared at their erections in awe. More heat spiked through her as she waited for them to touch her. Two gorgeous but drastically different men. Together they both wanted her, and everything she had dreamt of was coming true.

Quinn stepped in front of her and laced his hands through her hair. "You really have been such a good girl and I think you deserve a reward. Open wide, baby." He placed the tip of his cock against her lips and she opened her mouth, more than eager to taste him. She stroked the head of him with a long, slow lick before swirling along the more sensitive underside. His masculine heat and taste exploded on her tongue as she delved farther along the shaft with her mouth, his thick length stretching her lips around him. A deep, sexy groan from Quinn filled the quiet space of their apartment.

More. She wanted more.

So distracted by the luxurious feel of Quinn's dick in her mouth, she'd forgotten for a moment about Leo behind her until she felt the touch of a small, cool strip of leather against one bare ass cheek. He caressed circles along her skin and took his time going back and forth from one globe to another. His hand grabbed the rope that ran along her ass and pussy and she nearly came with a jolt.

She needed to beg again, but it was impossible to talk with Quinn's cock stuffed in her mouth, and his hands in her hair holding him all the way to the back of her throat. Katie relaxed her throat and did her best attempt to swallow against his flesh.

"Fuck!" His hands tightened in her hair and the muscles in his body visibly tensed. "Our little girl and her dirty little mouth are going to make me come soon."

She reveled in the pride his words gave her until a sharp crack across her bottom shot an intense piercing pain throughout her backside and straight to her clit. It hurt—oh God, it hurt— but damn if she didn't want him to do it again.

A deeper burning built in her womb as her inner muscles jerked in response. Before she could consider how to control it, another blow from the crop landed on the opposite cheek. Her mouth tightened around Quinn on a low, deep wail. He was going to make her come and she wouldn't be able to stop it this time. Pleasure seared through her until she thought she was burning alive.

"Oh yes, Katie, suck my fucking cock."

Spurred on by his words, she worked him harder and faster. Leo's hands did something with the rope behind her as it fell away from her pussy. The release of the pressure against her clit and ass should have given her a measure of relief, or an ability to control the building orgasm, but it didn't. It was too late.

Quinn thrust in and out of her mouth in a rapid, frenzied pace. Pushing his dick a fraction deeper in her throat each time. Pleased with the wildness of his actions and desperate to taste him, to have all of him inside her, she tightened her mouth and stroked her tongue at the same pace he fucked her mouth.

"Fuck. Yes. Baby!" His words were short and clipped with agony until she felt a blast of hot semen cross her tongue. She didn't—couldn't—stop or slow as she continued to suck him as he filled her mouth with his release, eager for every drop.

"My turn."

With one long and deep thrust, Leo plunged his cock into her juice-soaked pussy. She cried out around Quinn as she was stretched and filled to capacity. He immediately withdrew to the tip and sank back into her body with just as much force.

"Give it to us, Katie, it's ours. Your come is ours now."

She couldn't quite comprehend Quinn's words. Not with Leo's cock pounding into her, building an intensity that was completely out of her control.

"Say it, Katie," Quinn demanded

"Please. Please. I can't—"

"Say it or he'll stop."

Her body bucked with every stroke, and she was lost in arousal. Fingers touched her breasts, her back...everywhere.

"Ours." Leo snarled the word.

"Yes!" she screamed out to them, so desperate now. "Both of yours." A finger pressed against her clit and her body exploded.

Fracturing her into tiny bits of light and pleasure as her body rocketed against them in spasms.

Her legs and arms weakened, unable to support her any longer. She reached out for something to hold onto and grabbed the railing in front of her.

She cried out over and over again as the strongest release of her life quaked over her. Her pulse beat with the ever increasing volume of the music until finally a bit of reality began to sink in again.

Wait a minute. What am I holding on to? She pried her eyes open to find herself standing at the railing in the club. She glanced around to the hundreds of people around her. Most of them didn't see her, but a few watched her with curiosity, some with blatant desire if she wasn't mistaken.

Oh. My. God. No!

Heat and humiliation coursed through her as she realized that she had just orgasmed right here in front of all these people while lost in a daydream about Leo and Quinn. She wanted to run and hide from the embarrassment. How could this happen to her, she hadn't even been drinking.

Leo and Quinn.

They were just below her. She'd been watching Leo tie up another girl. She looked straight ahead at the stage, too afraid to look down. She had to get out of here. She would have to force herself to walk through the crowded club all the way to the exit and pray no one said a word to her. But first...she had to look down. Had to know if they'd noticed. Surely not. They were always so busy.

She took a deep calming breath and released on a nice slow exhale. She tilted her head down and looked. They both stood there, ropes in hand, staring up at her. Her gaze connected with Quinn and then with Leo. They both stared at her with such intensity and arousal that she thought the heat and embarrassment flushing her face would kill her.

Quinn was first to break into a smile. A grin so wide there was no mistaking just what they had witnessed.

Leo crooked his finger at her and motioned for her to come down. She wanted to duck and hide, but something deep within her wanted them more. She was a grown woman, and she could handle the fact that she had just had an orgasm in public. Hell, this was a fetish club, after all, and that kind of thing happened all the time here.

Just not to her.

She hesitated and Quinn's expression grew serious and mouthed one word to her. The one she'd waited for.

"Ours."

* * *

Thank you so much for reading!

Be sure to find out about new releases, deals and giveaways by hopping on my mailing list!
E.M. Gayle News.

Want to read Em and Rio's story in the next Purgatory Club book, WATCH ME?

Continue reading for the full first chapter of WATCH ME, which is available now. As well as an exciting sneak peek into another Purgatory series also available now!

If you're on Facebook or Instagram, come by and say hello! I'd love to hear from you.

If you enjoyed the story would you please consider leaving a review on your favorite retailer?

Just a few words and some stars really does help!

"Em, are you really going to go through with this?" Katie yelled over the loud music pounding through the club.

"Of course I am. It's what I've been working up to for months now. Why would I back out now?"

"Oh, I don't know. Because maybe when you take off that mask and Rio gets one look at the real you, you'll be a dead woman."

Em looked at her friend's frightened expression, trying not to laugh. It had taken a long time getting to know the people here at Purgatory before she'd built up the nerve to tell anyone who she really was. Now she was tired of hiding, and ready to unveil her identity once and for all. She didn't want to think about the public humiliation Rio could put her through if he made a scene. She worried too much about him as it was.

"You know they don't allow masks at the private after-hours party. If I want to take the next step in my journey, and I do, then I have no choice but to reveal myself. Rio be damned." If the man wasn't already damned. She looked up at where he stood, watching one of the play stations. Master D's station, of course. She couldn't tell what he was doing tonight, but she knew it was one of the more hardcore stations they offered where they did things like violet wand or needle play.

From this vantage point, she stared at Rio's profile. Wavy dark hair, tanned skin from working outdoors with her brother, and all black leather— from the vest to the pants that hugged what she knew was the most perfect ass on the planet, to the black leather boots he wore on his feet.

Here in this environment, he made it impossible to read his body language. She found him guarded, more often than not with a stern expression. Some went so far as to refer to him as El Diablo, the devil himself.

"Em, last dance of the night and I have a slot center stage with no one to fill it. You want it?" Gabriel, the club manager, had sneaked up behind her while she ogled Rio for the umpteenth time that night. She tore her gaze away and turned to Gabe with a smile on her face.

"You want me?"

"Ahh, my dear, you have no idea. Everyone wants the elusive Em."

"I find that hard to believe."

"Why is that?"

She shrugged. She wouldn't get into her insecurities with Gabe. Here in the club things were different for her. She wasn't the sweet little Emerson whom no one ever spoke to.

No, here she was bold and wanton, and reveled in the attention of the many patrons who liked to watch her. Even Rio. He'd been cool about it, of course, never showing too much interest, but there'd been a few times where she'd caught his gaze as he watched her play. She'd thought the heat in his eyes matched the arousal coursing through her body at his perusal, but so far he'd been aloof, never approaching her.

"So, darlin', do you want to take the chains?"

She'd been eyeing that platform for a long time, wondering what it would be like to get up there, helpless in front of everyone.

"Yes, actually I do." Already her body hummed with anticipation. What better way to kick off the rest of her night than by putting herself out there in a new way?

"Come with me then and I'll get you set up."

She followed Gabe through the crowd as they headed for the cage in the middle of the room. The energy of it all vibrated through her core, turning her on. She'd certainly come a long way from the first night she'd stepped into the club. Gabe held his hand up and she allowed him to lead her onto the small stage.

Her stomach tightened, partly from nerves, but mostly excitement. She looked down at her outfit, grateful that she'd chosen to go bold and daring tonight. The miniscule leather skirt didn't quite cover her ass, and the fishnet halter-top allowed a peek at her nipples that were currently straining against the fabric.

"Raise your arms for me, Em." She did as he asked and he placed the manacles around her wrists, fastening her arms to the chains hanging from the top corner of the cage. Emerson spread her legs and allowed him to fetter her ankles as well.

"You comfortable?"

She nodded.

Gabe stood back and appraised her appearance. "You picked the perfect outfit for tonight. If I didn't know better, I'd say you had something like this in mind to begin with." Heat flared in his eyes as he reached for the hem of her skirt. For a split second his fingers flirted with the crack of her ass before he rubbed his palms down the back of her thighs and up again, lifting her skirt to reveal her bare bottom and get the show started.

The crowd around her roared their approval as a shot of excitement rushed through her chest and straight to her clit. Large, strong hands massaged her ass as her body writhed in tempo with his movements. God, she loved this. Her head buzzed with the rhythm of the music and the heady sensations of Gabe stroking her ass while everyone watched and chanted for more.

When Gabe pulled his hand away she didn't expect the loud smack across her skin that came next. The stinging pain caught her breath until his hand returned and smoothed the pain away.

"I'll bet your pussy's soaked right about now."

"Maybe." Hell yeah, she'd felt a liquid rush from the moment she'd stepped up to the platform.

"Ahh, darlin', your teasing days are over now, aren't they? If you stay for the private session, one of these Doms here tonight is going to show us all just how tasty you are."

Emerson's muscles jolted deep inside her. Gabe had no idea how much she longed to take her education and experience to the next level. As much as she wanted Rio to be the one to do it, she wasn't waiting for him anymore. It was now or never.

Another resounding smack on her opposite cheek brought her focus back to the here and now, and the crowd cheering in front of her. Automatically her hands fought at the bindings around her wrists, her mind shrieking for her to touch herself.

"Everyone in the VIP area is watching you right now. Speculating...planning. But don't worry. Dan came up with the perfect idea for your introduction tonight. Something more civilized than just fighting over you." Gabe's breath tickled the back of her neck every time he spoke, only increasing the madness building inside her—and he knew it.

"Who is watching me?" She couldn't see the area behind her and she didn't have the guts to ask him if Rio watched.

"Everyone." With a final smack to her ass, Gabe strode from the platform, leaving her body on fire and pulsating with the music. Just the way the patrons liked it.

Emerson bucked and swayed her hips to the beat of the music as the image of Rio standing behind her, staring at her, burned into her brain. This wouldn't be the first time he'd seen her naked butt in the club, but it was the first time she'd gone to the cage to be chained. From everything she'd heard, that's how he liked his submissives. Chained and helpless...

* * * *

Rio watched the mysterious Em's slender body sway with the music, her pale skin glowing in the ultraviolet lighting. His pulse pounded through his veins to the same tempo, and his dick pressed against his zipper so tight he thought he'd probably end up with a permanent imprint.

His fingers itched to trace the curved lines of her back, feel her sleek skin against his own. There were so many things he could do to her in that position, all designed to maximize her pleasure and feed on the energy of the crowd. If she were his, he would keep her like that as often as possible —on edge, ready.

For weeks he'd watched her grow downright daring, noting the clothes she wore to the play stations she visited, and how she finally allowed herself to be restrained in performance. Several times she'd caught him, and he could have sworn desire and something more had flared in her gaze —the same arousal he experienced every time he caught sight of her.

It was a shame he couldn't see her luminous eyes right now, although his imagination could envision them quite well. Slightly parted lips and flushed skin topped off with a look of longing not even he could deny. With each slow roll of her hips and tug on the cuffs at her wrists, his mouth watered and more blood rushed to his groin. She looked hot on display—every man in the place watched her with obvious lust in their eyes and thoughts in their heads of what they'd like to do to her.

Mine.

She threw her head back, arching her neck, and thrust her breasts toward the crowd. Fuck, the woman would have him crazed with longing before this little show was over. In that moment, he longed to stand behind her, feel between her legs, and see for himself just how wet she'd become. To whisper in her ear how he ached to fuck her. But he wouldn't do it, not before she begged.

What about her drew him so much? He'd heard through talk about her age, which made him uncomfortable and had been one of the main reasons he'd avoided talking to her. His needs ran dark, and from his past actions he'd learned the inexperienced weren't likely to fulfill them. Now, watching her stand there bound and open, he wondered if he'd been too hasty in his assessment.

From this view he could no longer see her hiding behind her mask. He ached to see more of her like this, free and naked, waiting for him.

Yeah, he had it bad when it came to Em, the secretive little minx who riled everyone up without even realizing it. Something tugged at the edge of his conscious as he surveyed the scene. Gabe stood not far from the stage, keeping vigil over her, probably dying to get a piece of her for himself.

So with all the interested players and her willingness to put herself out there, why the mask? What could she possibly be hiding that couldn't be revealed here? Purgatory was all about being yourself, free to be who you needed to be. Not to mention taking the opportunity to indulge in some fantasies, no matter how forbidden.

Time was ticking and his patience would only hold out so long. Soon he would have to find out.

Read more now

LEVI'S ULTIMATUM

MASON'S RULE

GABE'S OBSESSION

GABE'S RECKONING

Purgatory Club:

ROPED

WATCH ME

TEASED

BURN

BOTTOMS UP

HOLD ME CLOSE

Pleasure Playground Series:

PLAY WITH ME

POWER PLAY

Single Title:

TAMING BEAUTY

WICKED CHRISTMAS EVE

WRITING AS ELIZA GAYLE

The Dragon Lore Trilogy:

THE CURSE OF THE DRAGON

THE SOUL OF THE DRAGON

THE FIRE OF THE DRAGON

Southern Shifters Series:

SHIFTER MARKED

MATE NIGHT

ALPHA KNOWS BEST

BAD KITTY

BE WERE

SHIFTIN' DIRTY

BEAR NAKED TRUTH

ALPHA BEAST

ONE CRAZY WOLF

Enigma Shifters Fated Mates:

DRAGON MATED

WOLF BAITED

BEARLY DATED

WOLF TEMPTED

Devils Point Wolves:

WILD

WICKED

WANTED

FERAL

FIERCE

FURY

Single titles:

VAMPIRE AWAKENING

WITCH AND WERE

Description:

One forbidden kiss. Two fractured lives. Sooo many secrets.

Maggie's obsession with the darker side of life has landed her in jail, in divorce court and now in the headlines of more newspapers than she cares to count.

She returns home to lick her wounds and reconsider her future, but just when she thinks her only solution is a tell-all memoir, a storm throws her in the path of the boy from her past. Except he's no boy. Nope. He looks like trouble and well, that's something she never can resist.

No stranger to scandal, Tucker's not going to let public opinion keep him from what he wants. He's getting his second chance whether she knows it or not. He'll open her eyes to the power, redemption and freedom that only he can provide. If she can let go of the past...

Tucker's Fall is the first book in a new series called Purgatory Masters. This is a spinoff from the Purgatory Club series that includes *Roped, Watch Me, Teased, Burn, Bottoms Up* and *Hold Me Close*. You do not have to read the Purgatory Club series first to enjoy Tucker's Fall, but once you experience Purgatory you might want to read them all.

Excerpt:

Tucker Lewis stared into the crowd and wondered when it would all end. He tightened his grip on the shot of Jameson and brought the glass to his lips. Across the bar and generous play space, fake smoke, dancers in chains, and throngs of half-naked partiers filled the club. The intense edge of the Lords of Acid music and the occasional scream of a submissive from the far side of the room fit right in with his dark mood. For better or worse this was the place he'd needed to be tonight.

The Purgatory club had come to be in a different life for him and the longer he sat here watching the scene around him; the less he believed he belonged. Of course his self-imposed exile hadn't helped much. He'd been riding high on life on borrowed time and didn't even know it. All it took was a simple house fire to bring his world crashing down.

"Wow, as I live and breath. Is that you, Tuck?"

Yanked from his mournful thoughts, Tucker focused on the man standing in front of him. Tall and imposing, he wore black leather that emphasized a gleaming baldhead that drew women of all ages. It didn't surprise him that his old friend from better days and one of the best damn rope riggers on the planet stood there with a smug grin.

"Fuck you, Leo."

"C'mon, Tucker. You know I'm not your type. But maybe this one is." Leo tugged on a leash he'd been holding and a very pretty redhead cautiously stepped out from behind him. Even with her eyes cast down, it didn't take much for Tucker to recognize her nervousness. Her hands intertwined with each other repeatedly as she shifted her weight from foot to foot.

Long, red hair brushed the tops of ample breasts that were barely hidden by a thin, black nightie that stopped before her thighs began. But it was the thick leather collar at her neck, branded with two names that stood out to him.

"I see things have changed for you since I last visited."

"Tends to happen when you disappear from the face of the Earth." Leo clapped his shoulder and took a seat on the bench next to him and his lovely submissive went to her knees on the floor at Leo's feet.

Tucker tried to ignore the slight pang inside him. It had been a long time since a submissive had caught his eye but that didn't mean the desire to have one of his own had completely disappeared.

"Will you introduce me to your lovely?"

Leo beamed. "Katie, say hello to Master Tucker. He's an old friend of mine."

With what looked like some reluctance, the little subbie lifted her head and met his gaze. "Hello, Master Tucker. It is nice to meet you." Immediately her eyes lowered back to the floor.

"You'll have to excuse Katie this evening. She's had a tough time with her commitments lately so Quinn and I have decided to devote this entire week to her correction." Leo stroked his pet's hair and brushed her cheek when she turned toward him.

The pang inside him clamored louder. The affection between Master and submissive was so obvious it was difficult for Tucker not to experience some degree of jealousy, although settling down had never been in his previous plans. "No need to excuse her. I completely understand." Maybe it was time to get back into the scene. He could meet a willing submissive here at the club and work out some of the kinks that had plagued his art this week.

"You thinking about rejoining us? Maybe some play tonight?"

Tucker shrugged, amazed Leo had read his mind. Tucker's body warred with his mind for control.

Part of him definitely needed to move on, but the other—well, he wasn't so sure.

"I'd be happy to offer Katie for service tonight. I think it would do her some good. She needs to get her head in the right place for everything she will be put through this week. What do you say?"

Tucker considered the offer while staring at the top of the pretty sub's head. She'd not uttered a word or made a move except for the tiny shudder he'd detected along her shoulder line when Leo offered her services. She impressed him and that wasn't an easy thing to do these days.

He stood from his seat and positioned himself legs apart in front of Katie. Leaning down he cupped her chin and titled her head back until her gaze met his. "I have a feeling I would enjoy your service very much."

She swallowed before a small smile tilted her lips. Whatever trouble she'd been having it was obvious how much she needed whatever Leo wanted to give her.

"It would be my pleasure, Sir."

A part of him really wanted to enjoy Katie. To take part in her discipline and let go of some of the stress he'd endured lately. His self-imposed exile needed to come to an end. He wasn't his father's son anymore. Unfortunately, his body had a mind of its own and wouldn't cooperate like he wanted it to. Flashes of another lovely lady filled his head. A woman he'd not actually laid eyes on in over fifteen years. Maggie Cisco. Professor. Newly single. Closeted submissive.

While he couldn't actually confirm the submissive part yet, his gut told him the truth. She'd been studying BDSM for so long there was no doubt in his mind there was a hidden ache behind her research. And he refused to entertain the alternative of her being a top. That didn't match the Maggie he knew from high school at all. Sure, people changed. He certainly had, but the fundamental core of who you are and what you need on a cellular level doesn't change in adulthood.

He'd bet every last dollar that Maggie possessed the heart of a true submissive, longing to take her place at her Master's side and he'd waited her out long enough. Her reappearance eight weeks ago had sparked more than gossip. Something inside him akin to hunger had unfurled and dug in with razor sharp claws and refused to let go. His recovery had taken a very long time. Too long. Now he needed to rejoin the world, engage in a healthy if somewhat temporary relationship and he'd chosen Maggie to do it with. She didn't know it yet, but he was coming for her.

Click here to read more now

The characters and events in this book are fictitious. Any similarity to real persons, living or dead, is coincidental and not intended by the author. The person or people depicted on the cover are models and are in no way associated with the creation, content, or subject matter of this book.

9 798201 127473